JACOB FLAX WITH ANGEL TURNER

Wichita Prairie Stars: The Rise

Marissa Boyd's Era

Second edition

This book was professionally typeset on Reedsy.
Find out more at reedsy.com

Contents

Author's Note

I authored Wichita Prairie Stars: The Rise in 2025. Knowing that I was to structure my soccer series for canon. Wichita Prairie Stars: The Rise is the first of this series. In the first trilogy, which will be the next two books along with this one, I wrote about a story about a women's soccer team that is based in Wichita called Wichita Prairie Stars. This work will cover: The Rise (this book), The Fall (the next book), and The Rise Again (the third book) Other books will be part of the canon.

Prologue: The Illusion of Success

The whistle tore through the heavy autumn air like a signal flare in the dark—piercing, absolute, and final. A stadium packed to its last breath exploded in a frenzy of noise, banners waving like a thousand beating hearts. The Wichita Prairie Stars had done it again. A third consecutive championship, this one clinched in the dying seconds of extra time, as if the gods of sport themselves conspired to write one more miracle in the book of Marissa Boyd. The field became a storm of motion—cleats thudding against turf, players collapsing in tears, coaches shouting with unfiltered ecstasy, and flashes from phones capturing moments already destined for legend.

Alyssa Garrett, drenched in sweat and joy, stood at the center of it all like a living statue carved from willpower. Her jersey, muddied and torn at the hem, bore the burden of a season's worth of sacrifice. As the league commissioner handed her the championship trophy, she lifted it high, and the gleam of gold under the floodlights cast radiant arcs over her teammates' faces. The crowd roared her name in waves—Garrett! Garrett! —but her gaze drifted to the sky, lips trembling with emotion. Beside her, Gabriela Hernandez sobbed openly, clutching the national flag over her shoulders, her hands shaking. This wasn't just a win. It was an affirmation.

Commentators on every channel scrambled to put history into words. KAKE's sports anchor, voice breaking, declared, "This is greatness cemented in eternity." ESPN ran a graphic: Three Titles. Two MVPs. One Dynasty. On ABC, a former Olympic player compared the Stars to the early U.S. Women's National Team— "Only with a tech-savvy twist and the heartland's steel," she said. The narrative was seamless, bulletproof. Here was the crown jewel of women's professional soccer, birthed in Kansas wheat fields and tempered in data labs and long nights. And behind it all, like the maestro of an orchestra no one dared question, was Marissa Boyd.

She emerged slowly into view, stepping out from the owner's suite and descending into the whirl of celebration below. Her silhouette was striking—a tailored cream suit, glossy boots, and the signature Prairie Stars lapel pin that had become a symbol of vision, of excellence. Cameras rushed toward her; microphones extended like offerings to a deity. She smiled, gracious but measured, as though fully aware of the myth she had authored and the careful balance it required. Commentators praised her with reverence, calling her "the godmother of the Silicon Prairie," a woman who had taken a failing team and built an empire.

"Boyd didn't just change a franchise," one analyst on ESPN said, voice reverent. "She rewrote the blueprint for women's sports in America."

They recounted her innovations: biometric tech to monitor player stress, a seamless fan-app that generated millions in microtransactions, and holographic community outreach programs. Her early investments in youth academies, her savvy signing of overlooked talent, and her revolutionary net-pay model that promised players higher take-home salaries than ever before. Her name had become synonymous with reinvention. She wasn't just an owner. She was a brand. A symbol. An answer.

And yet—when the cameras turned for just a moment—her smile faltered.

Marissa stepped briefly away from the crowd. She walked toward a narrow corridor behind the bench, away from the eyes and chants. A man in a dark suit handed her a folder, whispered something into her ear. Her eyes scanned the paper for a fraction of a second too long. Something in her jaw clenched. She nodded curtly, then turned back to the festivities. She smiled again. The mask realigned.

Elsewhere on the field, the celebration raged on, but cracks—small and nearly invisible—began to shimmer like stress fractures under polished glass. Elena Castillo, reserve player and once an intern during the first golden years, stood apart from the group, clapping with hesitant reserve. Her eyes weren't on the trophy or the fans. They were in a conversation between two board members, hushed and stiff. Gabriela, radiant under the spotlight, cast a brief, lingering look toward the VIP section. Her smile never dropped, but something in her posture shifted—a tension coiled in her shoulders like the ghost of a betrayal.

And standing just beyond the reach of the cameras, blending into the periphery of the frenzy, was Sara Trent.

Dressed in a charcoal-gray jacket and holding a discreet press badge, she observed like a hawk circling high above prey. While others shouted questions and exchanged pleasantries, Sara spoke into a discreet lapel recorder. "Event log, October 14th, 2033. Championship win. Mass euphoria. Public narrative intact. Boyd positioning secure... for now." Her eyes followed Marissa closely, noting the subtle body language, the moment of distraction, and the exchange of the folder. She flipped her pocket notebook open, making a notation in careful shorthand.

Trent didn't cheer. She didn't smile. She watched.

She had been watching for months now, monitoring financial flows, tracking shell entities, following silent leads from inside sources too afraid to speak openly. The pieces were still incomplete, but the shape they were forming suggested something monstrous beneath the gilded surface. Her sources spoke of double-booked payments, performance bonuses paid through crypto platforms, and a charity foundation whose tax filings didn't add up. None of it has been proven. Yet.

The camera drones ascended for the final aerial sweep, capturing the stadium in its full, electrified glory—flags waving, flares burning, confetti raining down in golden floods like divine approval. The perfect American dream. A midwestern empire built on belief, boldness, and data. Headlines would scream it in the morning: Three-Peat Queens! The Stars Shine Brightest!

But as the lens pulled back, farther and farther out, the noise began to fade. And in its place came something else: an almost imperceptible hum of dissonance. Boardrooms lit by cold LED light, tax documents lined with blurred signatures, encrypted messages flashing briefly across private screens.

And finally, a voice—Sara Trent's, filtered through a late-night podcast to a small but growing audience—asked the question no one dared:

"What if the Kansas Miracle isn't a miracle at all? What if it's a mirage?"

The screen went black. The illusion held—for now. But not forever.

1

The Kansas Miracle

T he Kansas Sports Equity Summit conference room was a gleaming temple of postmodern ambition, all glass walls, LED lighting, and hovering drone-cameras transmitting live feeds to thousands of investors, fans, and journalists nationwide. The scent of freshly brewed espresso lingered beneath the corporate polish, and all eyes were drawn to the woman in the power-blue blazer seated at the center of the stage. Marissa Boyd. Her name flickered across the digital banners like gospel—Architect of the Kansas Miracle. She sat with her back straight, her voice steady, her gaze immovable. You could mistake her for a seasoned politician or a Silicon Valley CEO, but she was neither. She was something rarer. A former collegiate midfielder from Iowa State with a knack for reading a game two steps ahead, who'd pivoted from cleats to code and built a mid-tier startup into a regional tech powerhouse before she was thirty. And now, she was the sole proprietor of the most improbable resurrection in American sports: the Wichita Prairie Stars.

The acquisition had been written off as another vanity project when it first broke in late 2027. The Prairie Stars were dead weight in the Women's United Soccer Alliance—a forgotten franchise losing games, fans, and millions in revenue. But Boyd saw something else. She described Inrly interviews with Forbes Sports as "an underused asset with untapped cultural equity." The media had run with it. Overnight, Boyd was recast as a disruptor, a visionary, a messiah for Midwestern women's sports. Her face lit up ESPN panels, TikTok entrepreneur reels, and #KansasMiracle trended before the Stars played a game under her leadership.

But behind every overnight success was a decade of preparation, and Marissa's was forged in silence. Flashbacks painted the picture: a young woman sitting alone in a university gym long after practice had ended, coding on her laptop while nursing an ankle injury. She learned the grit of sport and the logic of systems, and she applied both when reconstructing the Prairie Stars. League officials balked at her ambition. "You're not buying a team," one had said, jaw clenched over coffee in Chicago, "you're buying a carcass." Local business people shook their heads. "Soccer? Here?" Yet she pressed on, bulldozing doubt with sharp pitch decks and even sharper resolve.

She started with the players no one else saw.

Alyssa Garrett was a midfield dynamo from a Division II college in South Dakota—undersized, under-scouted, but with a mind like chess and a motor that never quit. Gabriela Hernandez had been tearing up training camps in Costa Rica, overlooked by scouts who were more interested in flashy agents than raw grit. Marissa brought them in not as filler, but as centerpieces. "I don't want stars," she told the press. "I want believers." Then came the innovations. GPS-enabled training vests, AI-driven nutrition plans, and mental resilience coaching apps. She partnered with local tech firms to outfit the team with gear that turned every scrimmage into a data harvest. Sponsorships followed—Midwest data labs, crypto startups, drone companies—turning the Stars' kits into neon testaments to the Silicon Prairie revolution.

And then, in 2029, the team did the unthinkable.

A playoff run.

The Stars went from bottom-feeders to dark horses, cutting through better-funded teams with precision and purpose. Wichita buzzed with electric pride. Restaurants painted stars on their windows. Game day foot traffic revitalized the struggling downtown corridor. The KAKE-TV evening broadcast declared it "the Boyd Effect," and national pundits weren't far behind. ESPN featured a segment called Heartland Glory. A Bloomberg anchor called it "the intersection of capital, community, and courage." At an economic conference that fall, Boyd stood beside the mayor and the Kansas governor as the Prairie Stars were celebrated as the blueprint for sports-driven urban revival.

But with success came scrutiny.

Boyd appeared on morning shows, business podcasts, and even at a tech conference in San Francisco, where she was asked how she achieved profitability so quickly. She smiled, delivering polished lines about lean operations, fan engagement, and agile payroll. The Prairie Star Foundation was unveiled next—an initiative for youth sports development in the region. But there were murmurs. The Foundation's website was vague, and its board was full of Boyd's former tech colleagues. Its donations flowed in, but where they went wasn't clear.

Late one night, the glow of the office lights bathed Boyd's angular silhouette in gold as she stood over a table filled with documents. A flicker of tension crept into her features. She flipped through a folder—tax codes, offshore compliance memos, legal advisories. Her general counsel, Dana Kellerman, a thin, sharp-eyed woman, hovered in the doorway.

"We'll need to restructure the Cayman funnel," Dana said cautiously. "The EU's tightening oversight."

Marissa didn't look up. "Then restructure it."

And deeper inside the team infrastructure, cracks began to show. Elena Castillo, a young Latina law student and reserve player interning in the operations office, noticed discrepancies, late bonus payments, and confusing contract language. When she asked the accounting lead about it, the answer came too quickly, too defensively. "Standard processing delay," he said, not meeting her eyes.

At a media conference in Kansas City, Sara Trent—a seasoned investigative journalist with a sharp pen and an even sharper gaze—stood to ask a question. Her voice cut through the applause.

"Ms. Boyd, can you comment on the structure of your net-pay agreements? Are they compliant with domestic labor laws and the league's salary cap regulations?"

Marissa responded with a smile that didn't reach her eyes. "We pride ourselves on innovation, Sara. Our athletes are compensated fairly and creatively."

The room chuckled, but Trent didn't. Nor did Marissa's assistant, who subtly clenched her notepad tighter.

As Sara walked away, her mind turned over details like puzzle pieces. Sponsorship deals that came from firms with no prior sports involvement. Payment ledgers that didn't line up with the announced figures. Her instincts prickled. The Kansas Miracle felt too clean, too fast.

The chapter's final image was grandeur—Wichita's new stadium glowing like a jewel under the night sky, filled with cheering fans. "Marissa! Marissa!" they roared as she took the stage. Drones hovered overhead, capturing every angle of this triumph.

And then, in a cut so sharp it might have drawn blood, the view shifted.

A dim office. A screen glowing with spreadsheets. Line after line of financial entries, red notations, flags, and footnotes. At the bottom, an innocuous code: EBT-INTNL-57.

Then, a voice—Sara's inner monologue—spoke softly over the image:

"Every miracle has a cost—it's just a matter of who pays it."

And so, the illusion began.

2

Financial Wizardry

I t began as a whisper—a clever idea spun into gold, marketed as innovation, and woven into the mythology of the Prairie Stars' rise. In early 2029, during a press conference held at a sleek, glass-walled venue just outside Wichita's downtown revitalization zone, Marissa Boyd unveiled the "Net Pay Model"—a revolutionary compensation structure she claimed would forever change the landscape of professional women's sports. Standing before a wall of Prairie Stars banners, Boyd's confidence glimmered beneath the soft camera lights, her tailored navy blazer as crisp as her rhetoric. "Our athletes deserve to keep more of what they earn," she declared, resonating with purpose. "We believe in financial dignity and smart compensation. We've simply optimized what others feared to question."

At first glance, Boyd's Net Pay Model was a beacon of hope. It promised a straightforward solution to the complex financial landscape of professional women's sports. No more navigating through multiple state taxes, bonuses clawed back by withholdings, or complicated filing regimes. It promised clean, straightforward deposits—no fuss, no uncertainty. Net pay meant what it sounded like: the amount you saw in your contract was the amount you took home. It sounded like magic. And in a league plagued by underfunded teams and archaic pay structures, it felt like salvation.

Analysts fawned. Kansas media outlets branded Boyd "the financial Elon Musk of women's sports." The Wichita Eagle ran a glowing op-ed titled Silicon

Prairie's Queen of Sports Finance. Nationally syndicated podcasts dissected her "forward-facing mindset," praising her tech background as the catalyst for this transformation. ESPN ran a late-night feature where a former sports exec commented, "This is what happens when brains meet bravery. She's not just building a team—she's building a legacy model."

But while the public bathed in the glow of Boyd's confidence, behind closed doors, her financial orchestra was composing something far more intricate.

The first crescendo came with the announcement of Gabriela Hernandez's arrival. The Mexican international, a striker with a blistering left foot and a magnetic fan presence, had long been a target of Europe's elite clubs. Yet, against every expectation, she signed with the Wichita Prairie Stars for a "record-breaking, player-first contract." During the press conference, Boyd stood beside Hernandez, hands clasped like a CEO unveiling a moonshot. "We didn't outspend anyone," Boyd said with a smile, "we outthought them."

While the fans erupted in praise and commentators hailed it as a masterstroke, behind the scenes, subtle currents of anxiety swirled. Agents began quietly asking each other: How is Wichita affording this? Financial advisors combed through the language of similar contracts. They noticed peculiar phrasing: deferred incentives linked to offshore metrics, third-party escrow disbursements, and clauses that shielded the team from direct responsibility for certain bonus payments. It didn't raise alarm—yet—but it didn't sit cleanly either. The unease was palpable, and suspicion was beginning to take root.

Then, without public explanation, the team's lead accountant, Thomas Weller, tendered his resignation. The sudden departure of a key figure in the financial team sent shockwaves through the organization, leaving many intrigued and questioning.

The official memo cited "personal family considerations," but those who worked with him noticed the change. His office, usually tidy and well-lit, had been dark in the weeks before his departure. The rumor—never confirmed— was that he had pushed back on one of Boyd's more elaborate payment flow structures and had shut swiftly. His replacement, a woman named Jeanine Lockhart, was introduced within days. A polished professional with a background in fintech compliance, Lockhart was efficient, loyal, and, above all, silent.

That silence grew louder over time.

In the months that followed, Boyd's financial strategy deepened. Through a series of shell entities registered in the Cayman Islands, the team's payroll and bonus structures began to flow through opaque intermediaries. Companies like "Alta North Consulting" and "Woolen Shore Holdings"—names that meant nothing on the surface—handled contract disbursements and deferred payments. To the players, the checks cleared. To the public, the Stars were thriving. But inside the finance team, the air grew colder.

A finance intern named Leah once asked why specific spreadsheets were stored on encrypted USB drives rather than the team's internal system. She was told, gently but firmly, to mind her lane. Another staffer reported delayed bonus disbursements after a player hit a performance clause—when he brought it up in a department meeting, Lockhart offered a tight-lipped response: "Banking delay. Don't worry about it." These instances raised concerns about transparency and the true nature of the team's financial operations.

Meanwhile, the culture within the organization began to shift. Questions became unwelcome. NDAs were expanded and reworded, particularly in sections referencing financial operations. Players were coached—subtly, but unmistakably—to value their take-home amounts rather than worry about "how" the money arrived. One assistant coach, overheard after a staff training, muttered, "It's like we're being told to love the cake and ignore the ingredients."

Boyd, for her part, remained untouchable. She gave interviews dripping with charisma, joined economic forums where she was praised as a disrupter of sports economics, and even accepted an award from the Kansas Chamber of Commerce for "Innovation in Professional Management." She smiled, toasted, and kept building.

And beneath it all, the groundwork for the EBT scheme quietly matured.

Deferred bonuses were tested first on foreign players whose tax liabilities were harder to trace. Funds were routed through consultancy firms that just happened to be run by former associates of Boyd's startup years. The contracts were legal, technically. But they were so carefully coded, so elegantly engineered, that even the league's compliance staff found little to object to.

Marissa Boyd had done the impossible. She had built a machine that looked like a team and moved like a movement. But beneath the gears was a delicate arrangement of smoke and wires, of off-system documentation, and quietly transferred liabilities. The players danced in the spotlight. The media drank from the chalice of her narrative. And the foundation—real one, unseen and unspoken—was poured in quiet rooms behind locked doors.

The miracle had a method.

And now, it also has a cost.

3

Under the Surface

I t began with a whisper—a digital murmur that echoed through the dark alleys of the internet. Sara Trent, an investigative journalist with a knack for uncovering political corruption, was engrossed in her home office one unremarkable Tuesday evening. She was reviewing notes for an upcoming feature on athlete mental health, not expecting any revelations that night. But when her inbox chimed and an encrypted ProtonMail message slipped through the screen, it took less than ten seconds for her instincts to sharpen. The subject line was deceptively simple: WPS // You Missed Something. But the attachment—a single spreadsheet file, embedded links, and a handful of unnamed shell entities—sent a jolt of anticipation through her veins.

At first glance, it was inconclusive: just names, figures, and Cayman Island addresses she couldn't immediately verify. But one thing gnawed at her— why would someone go to this much trouble for a hoax? Her experience told her otherwise. That night, long past the city's quiet fall into sleep, she cross-referenced the documents with the most recent tax disclosures from the Wichita Prairie Stars. And then she saw minor discrepancies in reported salaries, minute shifts between public contract announcements and what players had declared. The inconsistencies are too precise to be accidents and too consistent to be random.

Something was off.

By the following week, Sara had already begun building a web of names and accounts. She dug into old press releases, match-day programs, and publicly available contracts filed with the league. Player salaries were often touted proudly, especially for marquee signings like Gabriela Hernandez and the rising midfield star, Alyssa Garrett. But the numbers weren't aligning. Bonuses were either underreported or oddly staggered, and in some cases, players received lump sums long after they were earned, without any corresponding tax trail.

Sara picked up her phone and called an old acquaintance—Tracy Liu, a Kansas Department of Revenue compliance analyst. "I need an off-the-record check," Sara said, voice low. "Something doesn't smell right about the Stars. Their financials aren't matching their headlines." Cautious but intrigued, Tracy agreed to pull a few payroll reports and loop back with what she could find.

Meanwhile, within the tightly guarded walls of the Prairie Stars' newly christened training complex—Prairie Tech Arena—small unease tremors began to shake the ground beneath the pristine turf. The once serene atmosphere was now tinged with a palpable sense of unease, as if the very walls were whispering secrets.

Foreign players, especially those recruited last year from underfunded leagues in South America and Eastern Europe, began to notice something strange. Their contracts had guaranteed bonuses for appearances and goals, yet the payments arrived late, sometimes weeks past their due dates. When questions were asked, answers arrived polished but vague. "Banking delays." "International transfer compliance." "It's being processed through a trusted partner."

It was all said with smiles, but behind those reassurances, confusion brewed like a storm in the making, threatening to shatter the facade of trust.

Gabriela Hernandez sat in the locker room one afternoon after training, her brow furrowed as she scrolled through a banking app with a puzzled frown. "They say I got paid two weeks ago," she told her teammate, goalkeeper Lydia Jae, "but nothing's posted to my account." Lydia shrugged uncomfortably, glancing toward the hallway where staff might overhear. "It's probably just the system. You know how international wires can be." But Gabriela didn't answer. Her silence said everything.

In the quieter corner of the organization, reserve midfielder Elena Castillo—a law student by day and part-time player by ambition—was beginning to ask her own questions. It started as curiosity. She'd reviewed her latest contract while working on a class assignment about employment law. One clause caught her eye: compensation "may be subject to strategic disbursement under foreign performance protocols." That was strange. Another section mentioned third-party remittance services operating "on behalf of franchise subsidiaries." Subsidiaries? In what country?

The questions grew too loud to ignore. She met with her old professor, Dr. Mariana Ochoa, over coffee in Lawrence. "Can a U.S.-based employer legally route part of your salary through foreign shell companies?" Elena asked, pushing a printout of her contract across the table.

Ochoa read silently, her brow furrowing deeper by the line. "It's legal," she finally said, "but only if disclosed properly and structured transparently. This? This looks like someone hiding a house behind a hedge."

Back in Wichita, Sara Trent had started pulling on those hedges. A former Stars employee—someone close to the operations team who'd left quietly in early 2030—reached out with a message: "I have files. You didn't hear it from me." The files weren't complete, but they were damning enough. Company names are linked to bonuses. Cayman Island trusts. "Consultants" who signed off on performance clauses. The name "Alta North Consulting" appeared again—Sara had seen that once in the encrypted email. It was back, in internal documents routed through Jeanine Lockhart's desk.

Sara felt the trapdoor creak beneath the story she'd once seen only in highlight reels and ad campaigns. The narrative was twisting.

And still, the silence persisted, a heavy blanket of unanswered questions that seemed to stifle any hope of resolution.

The culture inside the Prairie Stars' headquarters had grown tense. Players were reminded not to discuss contracts. All staff were instructed to direct all media inquiries to the front office. And any internal audit requests were quietly shelved under "competitive confidentiality." Even team lawyers, once jovial and visible, had withdrawn into offices with locked cabinets and whispered meetings.

Sara and Elena, unaware of each other's parallel pursuits, were now tracing the same footprints through different corridors. Each had mapped networks of agents, shell entities, and suspiciously similar offshore addresses. Each had stumbled into a system engineered to deceive while dazzling the public.

And neither knew just how far down it went.

Inside the locker room, the air had started to change. Gabriela received another delayed payment and openly questioned the front office during a post-practice meeting. Always a team-first leader, Alyssa Garrett watched the exchange with quiet concern.

Outside, the fans still proudly wore their blue and silver. Marissa Boyd's face still appeared on digital billboards praising innovation and vision. The world hadn't seen the fissures yet.

But deep in her apartment, Sara began sketching her first deep-dive article, outlining what she now suspected was the story of a lifetime. Simultaneously, Elena sat at her laptop, constructing a timeline of her finances—each missing payment, every delayed bonus, each clause coded in ambiguity.

The illusion was beginning to peel.

And both women—unconnected, uncelebrated, and unstoppable-had just started the fire that would burn it all down.

4

The Web of Trusts

The façade of success had never gleamed brighter, yet beneath the surface, an intricate web was taking form—delicate in appearance but sharp enough to cut deep. As 2030 gave way to 2031, the financial wizardry once whispered in admiration began to ossify into something far more deliberate, far more dangerous. Marissa Boyd, the Silicon Prairie empress, was no longer simply a disruptor; she had become the architect of a shadow economy cloaked in the language of innovation. What began as whispered murmurs between lawyers and accountants had evolved into a fully-formed Employment Benefit Trust framework, its skeleton built on deferred compensation, shell entities, and global financial gymnastics most Fortune 500 firms would envy—and fear.

At its core, the EBT scheme was brilliantly sinister in its simplicity. Deferred player compensation—bonuses, performance incentives, even a portion of base salary—was routed through offshore trusts in the Cayman Islands. These trusts, bearing generic names like "Sunstream Capital Holdings" or "Palisade Reward Consortium," were registered to foreign post office boxes and overseen by law firms whose loyalty lay with dollar signs rather than jurisdictions. Third-party shell companies, often incorporated through international service providers in Belize or the British Virgin Islands, stood between the Prairie Stars and their financial obligations, giving the illusion that player payments came from the team and anonymous benefactors or consulting collectives. The bonuses arrived, yes—but routed through so many digital corridors and tax-neutral havens that their trail was nearly invisible.

For the players, it initially seemed like a dream dipped in gold. Boyd's financial team marketed the plan as "player-first innovation," with slick presentations emphasizing autonomy, higher take-home pay, and clever tax positioning. "We're simply doing what European clubs already do," Boyd would tell her stars with that signature blend of charisma and certitude. "It's all legal. Just smarter. More efficient. More... global." It worked. Gabriela Hernandez, the team's jewel, saw her bonuses nearly double in theoretical value. Alyssa Garrett, who had once quietly questioned her pay structure, now boasted of Prairie Stars' modernity on sports podcasts and postgame interviews.

Across the league, envy simmered. Players began requesting trades with Wichita for on-field excellence and paycheck engineering. Agents, sensing new profit channels, leaned in, their hands gliding over contracts rewritten with trust-based clauses and performance benchmarks calculated by foreign financial advisors. "It's revolutionary," one player agent told a Kansas City Star reporter. "Marissa Boyd has figured out the future of compensation." But no one—not the players, fans, or even the media basking in the Prairie Stars' glory—paused long enough to consider the cost of building such a future without a firm foundation.

Inside the front office, the atmosphere had begun to shift. What had once been a sleek, tech-savvy culture of empowerment now pulsed with something darker: complicity laced with quiet dread. Department heads who raised concerns were swiftly redirected, their objections silenced with revised job descriptions or quiet reassignment. Legal counsel updated boilerplate contract language, stripping away transparency in favor of abstract phrasing like "international disbursement conditions" or "benefit delivery partners." Those in the know simply stopped asking questions. Silence was easier than suspicion—and far safer. Even whispers between staff became measured, almost ritualistic. The culture, once anchored in progress, now revolved around protection.

For Elena Castillo, the warnings had started earlier and grown louder. She didn't carry the name recognition of Gabriela or Alyssa. She was a reserve midfielder, a scholar-athlete whose mind dissected footwork and federal codes with equal precision. When the numbers on her paychecks refused to align with the league's collective bargaining agreement, she felt a familiar twist in her gut—one born of legal textbooks and case precedents. At first, she assumed a clerical error. However, the more she reviewed, the more she saw discrepancies: overseas trusts cited in internal HR documents, irregular bonus timelines, deductions for "administrative holding periods" without any legal basis.

She brought her concerns to a trusted teammate—a quiet but sharp Canadian defender named Leah Dubois. Dubois had spent time with a union-backed club in Vancouver before joining the Stars.

"I'm not crazy, right?" Elena asked one day in the players' lounge, sliding a manila folder across the table, eyes darting to ensure they weren't overheard. "This clause here implies my bonus is subject to Cayman oversight. I didn't even sign anything about that."

Leah scanned the document, her lips thinning into a tight line. "It's not standard," she said, finally. "Not for league minimum. Not for anyone, really." She looked up, voice barely above a whisper. "Be careful, Elena. They don't like people asking questions."

And yet, Elena couldn't stop asking.

Trouble had already begun to show itself elsewhere, albeit in subtle, deniable ways. Bonus disbursements began arriving later. One foreign player found her performance payout chopped in half, without explanation beyond "exchange rate volatility." Internal accountants received vague directives to route certain funds through "external delivery mechanisms." Some offshore banks—particularly in Singapore and the Isle of Man—started requesting compliance clarification, subtly alerting Prairie Stars executives that their paperwork lacked the rigor required for international remittance. But rather than course-correct, Boyd's leadership team circled the wagons.

Meanwhile, a peculiar blog post appeared on Tax & Tactics, a niche financial site run by a retired hedge fund analyst. The piece, titled "Trust but Verify: The Curious Case of Prairie Stars' Compensation Trail," offered an eerily accurate speculative breakdown of how EBT schemes might be used to circumvent salary caps. It didn't name Boyd outright, but the implications were clear. The article gained little traction in the mainstream—drowned out by playoff hype and lifestyle interviews—but it rattled the small cadre of staff who had begun to suspect the truth.

Red flags started appearing in quiet succession within the Kansas state tax office. A junior auditor noticed discrepancies between reported incomes and high-value endorsements filed by Prairie Stars athletes. Another noticed withheld amounts that didn't match W-2 filings. By mid-2031, internal alerts had been logged, though no action had yet been taken, out of bureaucratic delay or deliberate hesitation.

Behind closed doors, Boyd doubled down. Staff were made to sign updated non-disclosure agreements with broader financial confidentiality language. Internal documents were scrubbed, redacted, or relocated entirely to off-system drives stored under "innovation privacy." Team meetings now included subtle reminders about brand loyalty, discretion, and the danger of "unnecessary transparency."

It was during this tightening of the screws that Sara Trent, still meticulously mapping the contours of her story, stumbled across something unexpected. While browsing a whistleblower forum commonly used by defense contractors and cybersecurity workers, she found a post titled: "Sports Shells: Offshore Patterns in the Prairie." The anonymous and articulate author outlined compensation practices eerily similar to what Sara had uncovered. The language was technical, but laced with outrage: "Deferred disbursements routed through Caribbean holding structures. NDAs enforce silence. Bonuses are delayed without clarity. Sound familiar?"

She reread the post five times, heart racing.

Across town, Elena Castillo sat in the Wichita Public Library's law archives, flipping through case studies on employee misclassification. Her phone vibrated with encrypted messages from a legal blog that had taken an interest in her anonymous inquiries.

The thread was tightening.

Neither woman could yet see how close they were to one another, nor how the trail they were separately following was beginning to bleed into the exact root cause. But both sensed the change. The illusion of invincibility was cracking, and quiet panic had started to take root among those who knew too much.

Elena closed her laptop that night with a decision that felt heavier than the keystrokes that made it: she would dig deeper, despite the risk.

Sara highlighted the forum post and whispered aloud to her darkened office, "Someone's finally speaking."

The web was tightening.

And no one, least of all Marissa Boyd, could stop it from being seen.

5

Golden Era on Shaky Ground

Autumn in Wichita was always crisp and golden, but the fall of 2031 shimmered with a brilliance few cities ever tasted. The Prairie Stars were untouchable—blazing through the league with an almost mythical rhythm, unbeaten in thirty-three straight matches. Fans packed the stands in a sea of silver and navy, waving flags that bore Alyssa Garrett's number like sacred symbols. Gabriela Hernandez, unstoppable and graceful, danced through defenders with the kind of brilliance that made even rivers weep. National media outlet observes *"The Kansas Dynasty."* *ESPN* aired an hour-long documentary called *Pride of the Plains,* while *ABC World News Tonight* opened a broadcast with drone footage of packed stadiums, weeping fans, and the Stars crest projected on the side of City Hall. It was more than soccer. It was a movement. A symbol. A miracle with a corporate logo.

Marissa Boyd, ever the conductor of this symphony, moved through galas and conferences like a queen in a digital age. She accepted awards with humble smiles and firm handshakes— "Innovator of the Year," "Visionary in Sports Finance," "Midwest Woman of Impact." Her speeches echoed across university stages and TEDx panels. *"This is what happens when you trust talent and embrace technology,"* she would say. In those moments, framed by soft lighting and applause, she didn't seem like a woman spinning plates. She looked like the safest bet in the American sports economy.

But behind the curtain, the sheen began to dull. Marissa Boyd, the mastermind of the EBT framework, was orchestrating a financial scheme that would soon unravel.

The financial office, once a hub of concern, has become a revolving door of quiet exits and cold silences. Boyd's original finance team—the architects of the EBT framework—was being methodically reshuffled. Titles changed, desks were cleared overnight, and new hires came in without so much as a public introduction. Communications from upper leadership slowed to a drip. Payments once delivered with the precision clock began to arrive later, smaller, and stranger.

The players noticed.

Whispers replaced locker room laughter. A few veterans swapped notes after practice, softly comparing payout dates. One foreign player, promised a loyalty bonus through an offshore "reward platform," confessed she hadn't seen anything in three months. Others murmured about contract adjustments— terms tweaked without formal notification, clauses moved from one page to another, legalese slithered into old agreements like ghosts. The Players' trust in the system was crumbling, and doubt, once planted, bloomed fast.

Alyssa Garrett, typically the bedrock of team morale, had begun her quiet inquiry. She was no stranger to contracts—her brother, a minor league baseball player, had once been financially burned, and she'd sworn she'd never make the same mistake. She pulled her original signing documents and compared them to recent pay stubs. Something didn't add up. Her bonuses, which were to be dispersed across performance thresholds, didn't match the agreement. A few had arrived late. Others were routed through unfamiliar institutions—offshore firms she hadn't authorized.

She brought it to the team's finance liaison. "There's probably just a temporary audit," the woman replied, eyes flicking a little too quickly. "You're getting what's due to you. It's just being... streamlined."

Gabriela Hernandez wasn't as patient.

After another missed goal bonus—her fifth of the season—she bypassed team protocol and requested a full audit of her compensation. The response compensation audit was from Boyd, but from a legal rep via encrypted email. It was bland and evasive, referencing "international delays" and "benefit distribution variances." Gabriela read it three times before storming out of the locker room. That night, she called an informal players' meeting.

After hours, they met in a Wichita cafe, blinds drawn, coffee cold in half-sipped mugs. Alyssa sat at the booth's corner; documents were folded beneath her hoodie. The conversation was hushed, intense, interrupted only by worried glances toward the door. "This isn't just delays," Gabriela said. "Something's being hidden. Our money's not where it's supposed to be." A rookie asked whether they should contact the players' union. Another, quieter voice in the back asked, "Would they even believe us?" But one thing was clear–they were united in their determination to uncover the truth.

Meanwhile, Boyd carried on the public show with breathtaking precision. She gave interviews on *Bloomberg Sports*, launched a new fan engagement platform, and smiled through staged photo ops with local officials discussing Wichita's economic boom. But inside her private office, the pressure had begun to mount. The Cayman trusts had started asking questions—documents needed clarification, fund transfers were flagged, regulators in Singapore were no longer satisfied with "deferred bonus consultancy." Marissa pushed back, demanded speed from her intermediaries, and revised contract pipelines. She kept the illusion intact, but the machinery was overheating, and the strain became increasingly palpable.

Her investors had begun asking questions too—not in front of the cameras, but over private lunches and encrypted calls. *"What's the long-term cash position?" "Can these bonus structures scale without new capital?" "When will we see a return?"* She gave them reassurances with a vision. But in the pit of her stomach, she knew the math was no longer magic. It was a maze. One, she was now racing to navigate blind.,

And through it all, Elena Castillo watched.

She had grown quieter, more careful, and infinitely more dangerous. Now fully aware of the EBT structure and how it fed through every inch of the Prairie Stars' payroll, she began to journal—first in vague notes, then in exacting detail. Each discrepancy. Each late deposit. Each clause that mutated without notice. She reviewed other players' concerns with calm empathy, storing them like puzzle pieces. Her legal training told her what she saw was more than unethical—it was illegal. Misrepresentation, offshore deception, and selective disbursement. The floor was not just red. They were burning.

But Elena wasn't ready to move yet. Not until she had everything.

And just across the city, Sara Trent was beginning to sense the coming college-banked envelope had arrived at her office—inside, documents from someone deep within the organization—financial charts, internal memos, and a financial dribble in black ink: *"You were right. It's a house of cards."*

That weekend, Sara attended a Stars home game under the guise of covering the playoff race. The stadium pulsed with energy, the crowd was in full voice, and the team played with the same fire that the team played with. On the surface, everything was perfect.

But Sara didn't look at the field.

She watched the bench. The staff. The executives in the glass suite.

She watched Marissa Boyd.

And in her mind, the article began to write itself—not as a celebration, but as an obituary for an empire built on illusion.

The spectacle was magnificent.

But the storm was already here.

6

Cracks Appear

This kind of discovery made Sara Trent stop breathing for a moment. Late in the evening, her office bathed in blue monitor glow, she stared at a spreadsheet assembled from a patchwork of internal emails, tax disclosures, offshore registry leaks, and cross-referenced banking trails. The lines told a quiet story—one without headlines or confessionals—but it was damning nonetheless. At the center of it all, beneath the layers of trust entities, consultant firms, and foreign financial proxies, was a name: *Marissa D. Boyd.*

The connection was no longer theoretical.

Using leaked documentation—some anonymous, others provided by a growing network of disillusioned insiders—Sara traced direct ownership links between Cayman-based trusts and Boyd's financial shell, *Prairie Horizon Holdings.* That entity, once described as an "innovation incubator," was quietly funneling performance bonuses to players through tax-neutral vehicles registered under different names but governed by contracts Boyd had personally countersigned. The elegance of the deception was as brilliant as it was fragile. It had lasted this long because no one dared imagine someone so public and polished could be operating with such duplicity.

Sara printed the diagram. A simple web of arrows and red lines connecting Boyd's official title to foreign accounts, shadow firms, and bonus disbursements. At the bottom, in Sara's careful script, were the words: *"It always leads* home."

But just as her investigation reached its crescendo, the dam finally broke.

As the investigation reached its crescendo, the dam finally broke. That night, a whistleblower uploaded Gabriela Hernandez's contract to a secure leaks forum. By morning, it had gone viral. Sports journalists, financial analysts, and legal experts pounced on the leaked document like a dropped pearl in a temple. What began as a trickle of curiosity soon erupted into a storm of national speculation. The public scrutiny was relentless, and the document only confirmed what insiders had long whispered: Gabriela's base salary was modest, but layered with offshore incentives routed through two named entities—*Sunstream Capital* and *Meridian Trust Group.* Her tax declarations didn't list either. The contract included language about "international performance acceleration" and "conditional deferred equity," terms unheard of in league-standard agreements.

Cable sports shows scrambled to cover the leak. ESPN's *First Take* opened with:

"Is the Kansas Miracle a Mirage?"

A talking head on *Good Morning America* asked bluntly, "How much of Gabriela's money is real, and how much is... smoke?"

In Wichita, the illusion that had charmed an entire region began to splinter. KAKE was the first local outlet to pick up the leak with any investigative seriousness. Their *"Contracts and Questions"* report aired that evening with a quiet urgency. Using accessible language, they walked viewers through the Cayman trust model and how such a structure could—intentionally or not—skirt taxation and financial transparency laws. They ended the segment not with conclusions, but with a haunting question: *"If this is how they pay one player, how many more contracts look the same?"*

Quietly, the Kansas Department of Revenue launched a tax review into the Prairie Stars organization. A unit specializing in irregular income patterns began combing through player filings, cross-referencing deposits, endorsements, and fringe benefits. On the surface, they moved cautiously—an inquiry, not yet an audit. However, within internal memos, the tone was different. *High-risk structuring. Low visibility. Political sensitivity.* A profile was being built, leading not just to Boyd, but to an entire system that had seduced accountants, sponsors, and a league office that hadn't looked closely enough.

Inside the locker room, the tension was palpable. Gabriela's refusal to comment on the leak spoke volumes, her body language a silent accusation—arms folded during team talks, eyes hard as flint during post-match interviews. Alyssa Garrett, usually composed, was now seen reviewing her documents under the low hum of fluorescent lights in the training facility's player lounge. Younger teammates whispered after practices, their trust in their contracts shaken. The once harmonious locker room was now a place of suspicion and doubt.

Sponsors, once the Stars' most loyal chorus, began to express concern behind closed doors. A regional bank asked for a meeting to "clarify exposure." A local construction firm delayed a promotional rollout. The cracks were now visible to anyone who chose to look.

And finally, after months of silent conviction and restrained observation, Elena Castillo made her move.

She found Sara Trent's contact through an encrypted source verification program and sent a discreet message, encrypted end-to-end. The message read simply:

"I know what's happening. I've seen the documents. I have more."

They met not in an office or newsroom, but in the back of an old law library, where the dust seemed to listen as well as any confidante. Elena brought folders and notes, copies of contracts and timelines, a notebook filled with dates, acronyms, and payout figures. As Sara leafed through the materials, the silence between them turned electric. They were no longer working in parallel. The tracks had merged.

Together, they mapped what they now understood to be a layered, deliberate, and deeply illegal operation, disguised by Boyd's charisma and cloaked in her team's on-field brilliance. They coordinated secure drop locations, burner devices, and private legal consultations in case retaliation came swiftly. They tightened the snare with every document they uncovered and every timeline they aligned.

Meanwhile, Marissa Boyd responded publicly, calm, composed, and immaculate. She addressed the leak with masterful deflection at a hastily arranged press conference following practice. "The details of Gabriela's contract are being taken wildly out of context," she said, standing before a backdrop of sponsor logos and smiling teammates. "We have always complied with local and league regulations. The focus now should be on our historic season, not fear mongering."

But even her tone had shifted. Gone was the carefree innovator. In her place stood a CEO in defense mode—measured, practiced, and beginning to show the strain.

The press didn't buy it. Fans weren't sure.

That night, as Sara sat in the bleachers of a half-filled stadium watching another Prairie Stars victory, she noticed something no one else did: the applause felt different. Lighter. Slower. The chants are less unified. Something sacred had been fractured. She looked down at her notebook, the phrase "house of cards" circled twice. The stadium lights bathed the players in gold. But for Sara, it felt like the glow of a dying star.

The truth had a pulse now.

And it was getting louder.

7

Whistleblower

The wind was sharp that evening, slicing through the quiet campus of the University of Kansas with the bite of late November. Inside the dim legal archives building, where overhead lights flickered with the fatigue of overuse, Elena Castillo sat alone—her laptop open, her fingers trembling ever so slightly as she scrolled through the last of the documents. The file she had just opened wasn't supposed to exist on the team's internal drive. Labeled *"Confidential Risk Memo: EBT Structuring and Legal Exposure,"* it bore the signature of the Prairie Stars' legal counsel, and what it contained chilled her more than the wind ever could.

Within its densely worded paragraphs, one truth screamed with undeniable clarity: *they knew.* In clean legalese, the memo acknowledged that the ongoing use of offshore Employment Benefit Trusts carried *"non-trivial risk of criminal tax exposure"* and could constitute *"federal wire fraud under certain interpretations if not properly disclosed to recipients and tax authorities."* Footnotes cited IRS precedent, internal discussions referencing outside counsel's hesitations, and emails quoted from Marissa Boyd—emails where she insisted the team remain "agile" in its compensation strategy despite "regulatory noise."

Elena's internal turmoil was palpable as she leaned back, hands rising to cover her mouth. Her heart pounded not from surprise but from confirmation. She had suspected. She had feared. But now she *knew*. And she knew that keeping silent would no longer make her innocent. In the eyes of the law, continuing to accept payment through those structures made her complicit. She wasn't just a reserve player anymore. She was part of a conspiracy.

But more than law, it was conscience that gripped her. The long nights of unease, the moments she'd stayed after practice, flipping through legal textbooks under the hum of fluorescent lights. The hushed conversations with classmates about whistleblower statutes. The ethics seminars were where her professors spoke of obligation, of the higher duty owed when law and loyalty clashed. Flashbacks stirred like specters—her first season, wide-eyed and grateful, trusting every document handed to her; the first time she noticed a deposit routed through a bank in Liechtenstein; the first time she asked a question and got nothing but a smile and a clipboard.

Now it was too late to pretend. She was standing at the edge of a line she could no longer avoid crossing.

That night, shrouded in the safety of darkness and buried under layers of security protocols, Elena Castillo made her choice. She connected to the university's encrypted legal research network, downloaded a burner VPN, and began compiling the most dangerous package she would ever assemble. Dozens of documents—payment records, trust formation files, internal memos, routing numbers, legal correspondence—all meticulously organized into a digital dossier. She formatted the files into an anonymous submission and routed them through multiple secure drop points.

The final email went to the Kansas Department of Revenue's Financial Crimes Division and a high-level intake portal within the Internal Revenue Service.

She never signed her name.

Within twenty-four hours, the gears of government began to turn.

It started small, almost imperceptibly—a flagged report at the state level, a request for interagency coordination. Within a week, the Kansas DOR initiated a formal investigation under quiet status. The IRS followed suit, assigning two forensic accountants and an attorney to liaise discreetly with state officials. These movements were silent, buried under layers of bureaucratic protocol, but the vibrations were felt almost instantly inside the Prairie Stars' corporate structure.

The legal team caught wind of something—a data request here, a subpoena whispered there. Nothing was confirmed, but paranoia metastasized. Boyd responded with swift severity. Internal communications were further locked down. "Data protection consultants" were brought in—ostensibly for cybersecurity, but their real job was clear: root out the leak. Team phones were audited. Communications were flagged. Boyd didn't speak publicly, but privately, her fury was volcanic.

"We've been compromised," she told her CFO in a hushed hallway. "Find out *who*."

Overnight, the atmosphere inside the locker room underwent a dramatic shift.

Trust evaporated. Players whispered in corners. The camaraderie of seasons past dissolved into side glances and suspicion. One foreign midfielder stopped speaking during meetings entirely. A veteran forward abruptly requested a trade. Gabriela Hernandez, once the unshakable face of the team, now carried herself with a guardedness that even the media couldn't miss. The club gave no public explanation, but *KAKE*, *The Eagle*, and *ESPN Midwestern Sports* all began running speculative headlines:

"Trouble in Paradise?"

"Rifts at the Top of the Prairie Stars Dynasty?"

Elena became a ghost in her locker room.

She was still present—technically still part of the team—but increasingly sidelined. Coaches offered vague reasons: "tactical rotations," "player development." She wasn't included in training simulations. She wasn't on the travel roster. And off the field, her isolation was palpable. Teammates who once smiled now avoided her. Conversations stopped when she entered the room. She could feel the suspicion—not confirmed, not voiced—but *there*, growing like smoke before a fire.

She bore it in silence. Every moment, a tightening vice on her nerves.

But she never regretted it.

Late at night, in her dorm, she kept a second journal—not one of her legal studies or tactical diagrams, but a record of the unraveling. A first-person archive of fear, of ethical conviction, of betrayal, of duty. She wrote not just for herself, but in case her name was ever revealed, so there would be no mystery about why she did it. So that the record would speak, even if she couldn't. Her determination to maintain her integrity was unwavering.

She maintained contact with Sara Trent, albeit carefully. She passed along updates through secure messaging and cloaked addresses: locker room mood, administrative shifts, whispers from within. Now fully aware of the storm about to break, Sara prepared the following article with surgical precision— fact-checked, verified, and timed with perfect restraint.

The team continued to play, but something fundamental had shifted. On the field, they were slower and less unified. In one critical late-season match, a missed penalty led to a sideline shouting match that the cameras couldn't ignore. The media ran with it. Pundits speculated. But no one, outside the circle of truth, knew just how far the rot had spread. The weight of their actions was palpable, and the team struggled to bear it.

Elena knew.

And as the season spiraled toward its bitter end, she looked up at the sky one afternoon after practice, its grey expanse stretching endlessly above the flat Kansas plains. She breathed deeply. The storm was coming.

And when it hit, it would have her name in its wake.

8

The Eagle Has Landed

O n a cold, bright Monday morning in February, a single headline crashed the illusion.

"*Prairie Mirage: The Financial Web Behind America's Soccer Dynasty*" —by Sara Trent. The title, 'Prairie Mirage', alludes to the deceptive nature of the financial operations behind the seemingly prosperous 'America's Soccer Dynasty'.

It exploded across the digital front pages of *ESPN*, *ABC News*, and Wichita's *KAKE-TV*. The article spanned twenty thousand words, a sprawling, surgical exposé unmasking the clandestine empire Marissa Boyd had spent nearly six years constructing in the shadows of glory. Names were named. Trusts were traced. Contracts were dissected line by line. Once heralded as a genius innovation, every layer of the Employment Benefit Trust scheme was now exposed as a dangerous dance of deferred compensation, Cayman shadows, and federal deception.

Sara Trent had waited for the perfect moment. With the Wichita Prairie Stars charging into the new season undefeated and morale riding high, she dropped her bombshell just as fan engagement reached its annual peak. The result was nuclear.

Within hours, #PrairieMirage trended on X, TikTok, and Instagram. Thousands of fans, many in utter disbelief, flooded comment sections with outrage, questions, and grief. Former league officials tweeted cryptic acknowledgments of prior suspicions. Sports podcasts halted their pre-planned segments to dive into the revelations. KAKE-TV led its 6 p.m. newscast with drone footage of PrairieTech Arena, its pristine walls now surrounded by protestors bearing signs that read *"Boyd Lied"* and *"Trust in Truth, Not Trust Funds."*

At first, the national conversation fractured along familiar lines. Some pundits accused regulators of overreach. Others claimed Boyd was a victim of success, punished for daring to challenge the old guard. But that narrative didn't last. The facts—evident in Sara's meticulous reporting—were too damning, too vivid, too well-documented to be ignored. When the article laid bare how players' earnings had been siphoned through shell companies named after ocean birds and mineral holdings, public sympathy drained fast. When readers saw the diagram of offshore routing systems shaped like a financial spiderweb, something broke. The public's reaction was intense, to say the least.

And then came the real storm.

The IRS formally announced a joint investigation with the Kansas Department of Revenue into the financial operations of the Prairie Stars, naming Gabriela Hernandez and Alyssa Garrett as two key figures whose contracts were under forensic review. Subpoenas flew like arrows. The league, blindsided and bruised, announced a parallel compliance review, forced to reckon with years of regulatory neglect. Tax experts on CNN and CNBC began walking through just how illegal the "compensation innovation" might be, with some describing it as *"a case study in corporate evasion wrapped in sports heroism."*

The world was watching now.

Marissa Boyd did not flinch—at least not in public.

Two days after *Prairie Mirage* detonated, she sat poised across from a primetime anchor on *ABC Nightline*, her expression a portrait of defiant elegance. Dressed in all black, with her Prairie Stars pin still fastened to her lapel, she smiled calmly, even as the anchor read damning lines from the article.

"Our compensation system is unconventional," she said, "but it's not illegal. What we've done is create an opportunity for players, women's sports, and the Midwest. These attacks? They're driven by fear. Fear of change. Fear of a woman building something bold. Boyd refers to the 'compensation innovation' system that allegedly funneled players' earnings through shell companies and offshore routing systems, a practice that some experts describe as 'a case study in corporate evasion wrapped in sports heroism.'

Behind the scenes, she was in full damage control. Legal teams were ordered to delay, defer, and discredit. NDAs were reinforced. Staff were instructed to refer all questions to a "crisis response unit." Privately, she demanded that internal communications isolate the whistleblower, whom she now suspected resided within the player ranks. The 'whistleblower' is an individual within the team who allegedly leaked information about the financial scandal, causing Boyd to intensify her efforts to identify and silence them. "Find the leak," she hissed during a closed-door meeting. "And end it."

Meanwhile, the locker room became a war zone of whispers and widening fractures.

Training camp was chaotic. Media vans swarmed the stadium gates, and security lines wrapped around the perimeter. Reporters hounded players on their way into workouts, their faces caught in lenses and flashes. No comment became the anthem of survival.

Inside, trust—so critical to any team's chemistry—had shattered. Some players rallied around Boyd, convinced they were victims of sensationalism. Others, led quietly by Alyssa Garrett and Gabriela Hernandez, pulled away. Already burned by the leaked contract scandal, Gabriela stopped attending team dinners. Alyssa, once Boyd's most vocal advocate, skipped a charity gala for the first time in four years. Tension thickened every conversation. Arguments, once rare, now erupted over drills and substitutions. Teammates began refusing media interviews altogether.

And then the sponsors began to vanish.

A regional bank paused its contract, a major apparel brand suspended all joint promotions, and a national cereal company pulled out of a Prairie Stars-themed marketing campaign mid-production. Local businesses that had once wrapped their storefronts in silver and navy began peeling decals off their windows. Ticket sales dipped, and merchandise tables at games stood half-stocked and mostly untouched.

Outside the stadium, fan protests grew in size and intensity. Banners waved in the cold Kansas wind—*"Boyd Lied. We Paid."* and *"Not Our Dynasty."* On social media, clips of fans burning Prairie Stars jerseys in trash bins played to haunting violin music. A mural of Boyd downtown was defaced with red spray paint reading: *"Mirages Fade."*

But in the center of this maelstrom, Sara Trent soared.

The exposé catapulted her into the national spotlight. Interview requests poured in from every major network. *60 Minutes. PBS Frontline. NPR's Morning Edition.* She declined many, choosing carefully, always speaking in measured tones. She didn't gloat. She didn't claim vindication. "This was never about destroying a team," she told one interviewer. "It was about unveiling a truth that was hidden beneath the noise of success."

She hinted—just barely—at more revelations to come. An entire book, she said, was in progress. It would go deeper. Touch names not yet printed. Shine lights into the final corners.

The opening weeks of the 2033 season limped forward. The team that had once radiated invincibility now looked fractured and uncertain. Players looked over their shoulders as often as they looked at the goal. The roar of the crowd was no longer celebratory—it was interrogative. The uncertainty of the team's future hung in the air, creating a palpable suspense.

And somewhere, in the stillness between legal subpoenas and halftime whistles, a truth settled over Wichita like a silent snowfall:

The Eagle had landed.

And the fallout had only just begun.

9

Legal Storm Clouds

By June 2033, the bright, aspirational veneer that had cloaked the Wichita Prairie Stars for nearly six years had been stripped to the bone. The fortress Marissa Boyd had meticulously engineered—a symphony of silver banners, tech-forward PR, and financial prestidigitation—was now ground zero for one of the most aggressive financial investigations in American sports history. The IRS no longer dealt with polite queries or quiet requests. They arrived with subpoenas. The Kansas Department of Revenue also had investigators armed with court orders and long lists of names.

Every spreadsheet, payment ledger, and boardroom memo that had once existed in the shadows was now subject to forensic scrutiny. The documents spanned hundreds of pages: coded offshore transfers, manipulated bonus schedules, and internal discussions openly weighing "regulatory blind spots" as a business strategy. The regulators weren't asking anymore. They were assembling.

And then the storm turned personal, tearing at the fabric of trust and loyalty that had bound the team together.

Elena Castillo's name was leaked to the press—not through her choosing, but through an unnamed source close to the Prairie Stars' executive circle. Within hours, her identity as the whistleblower broke across multiple platforms, and she became the most polarizing figure in Kansas sports history. At first, the backlash was swift and brutal. Anonymous accounts bombarded her social media with venom. A few players—frustrated and fearful—made passive-aggressive remarks during post-practice interviews. One unnamed teammate told a reporter, *"Some of us believe in loyalty. That's all I'll say."*

But something strange began to happen.

Public opinion began to shift—not in one sudden wave, but in slow, tidal turns, creating a sense of unease and anticipation. Interviews with former interns, backroom staff, and even a junior accountant echoed Elena's concerns. Legal analysts explained whistleblower protections and the moral duty to expose criminal conduct. And then came *The Interview*—a quiet, intensely personal conversation between Elena and Sara Trent, aired late at night on ABC. Filmed in soft lighting with no studio audience, Elena spoke not as a crusader but as a young woman wrestling with the weight of what she'd uncovered.

"I didn't want to destroy the team," she said, voice steady but cracked with emotion. "But I couldn't live with the lie. Not when I knew what it meant."

The public saw her not as a traitor, but as a truth-teller.

Days later, another leak detonated across the media landscape—internal board minutes from a 2031 meeting where Marissa Boyd and her senior advisors discussed "offshoring exposure risk" and "leveraging player trust to enable cross-jurisdictional bonus dispersals." The language was damning, and the tone was cold. One executive had even joked, *"Trust them with Trusts—literally."*

The leak included hundreds of pages of correspondence, including emails in which legal counsel raised red flags and were ignored, Slack messages discussing "how far we can push Cayman," and a PowerPoint slide labeled *"Layered Compensation Strategy—Internal Eyes Only."*

#TrustGate exploded across social media.

Memes mocked Boyd's now-infamous quote about "financial dignity through innovation." Protesters camped outside PrairieTech Arena with signs that read *"Transparency or Bankruptcy"* and *"Miracles Don't Lie—People Do."*

At the heart of the chaos stood Gabriela Hernandez, who had recently been seen as the crown jewel of Boyd's empire. Her name, record-breaking contract, and meteoric rise were now case studies in the scandal. *The New York Times* ran a feature titled: *"Icon or Instrument? The Gabriela Question."* In it, financial documents showed how her compensation had been structured through three-layered trusts, routed through Belize, and partially paid in cryptocurrency linked to a now-defunct European consultancy.

Gabriela released a carefully crafted statement via her publicist. It was measured, mournful:

"I am shocked and saddened by what I have learned. I trusted that all agreements made on my behalf were in full legal and ethical compliance. I no longer feel that trust was earned. I stand with those seeking transparency and accountability."

The impact was seismic. Her departure from the Boyd camp signaled a turning tide.

Sponsors fled in droves, and local businesses canceled partnerships. One Wichita radio station began boycotting Star's content altogether. Merchandise sales plummeted by 60% in weeks, and even long-loyal fans turned their backs—some literally—during home games. The stadium was no longer a temple of dreams. It was a war zone of truth.

Meanwhile, Marissa Boyd prepared for battle.

She retained a white-shoe law firm from New York, staffed with federal litigation veterans and offshore financial specialists. She made cryptic public remarks, accusing the media of "waging an ideological war against female-led innovation." In a tense press conference, she refused to acknowledge wrongdoing, instead citing "competitive sabotage," "political timing," and "jealous rivals hiding behind bureaucrats."

But the legal pressure was mounting fast. Grand jury whispers began circulating in D.C. Legal analysts filled evening panels, listing off charges that could now be in play: tax fraud, wire fraud, misrepresentation, conspiracy, obstruction. A former federal prosecutor told MSNBC, "It's no longer about if charges come. It's about how many."

Inside the locker room, morale collapsed.

Training sessions became battles of silence and sharp looks. Players who sided with Elena were iced out by those still loyal to Boyd. The head coach tried to hold team meetings—tried to unite—but no message of unity could survive in an environment riddled with fear and fatigue. "We're playing two games now," he confided to an assistant. "One on the pitch. One in court."

Alyssa Garrett, once the team's moral center, had stopped speaking to Boyd altogether. She stayed late after practice, often alone, working through drills, not out of passion but as an escape. The game was no longer a joy. It was survival.

As the investigations deepened, financial instability loomed. Several board members held emergency meetings, whispering about cash reserves, potential legal exposure, and liability insurance that might no longer exist. Restructuring was now a whispered inevitability, and bankruptcy protection was a card on the table. All the while, Boyd clung to her myth with crumbling fingertips.

Boyd sat in her glass-walled office above PrairieTech Arena, staring at a financial report splashed in red ink. Outside, protestors' chants echoed off the building like thunder. She raised a trembling glass of whiskey to her lips and whispered, "Let them come."

She no longer controlled the narrative. The house she built was collapsing. And the end had only just begun.

10

Chapter 11 Filing

The air outside the Sedgwick County Courthouse was thick with tension and microphones. Reporters elbowed each other for space as a cascade of camera flashes painted the gray autumn sky with artificial light. At precisely 11:03 a.m., a black sedan pulled to the curb. Marissa Boyd emerged—not in the sleek designer suit that had once defined her public persona, but in a stark charcoal blazer, devoid of adornment, her expression steel-forged and unblinking. She walked past the reporters without flinching, a single folder tucked under her arm, the weight of a broken empire folded between its pages.

Moments later, the official announcement hit every screen in America: *Wichita Prairie Stars File for Chapter 11 Bankruptcy Protection.*

The woman who once built an empire on promises of innovation, technology, and financial acumen now stood at the precipice of total collapse. Boyd's voice was hard, clipped, and deliberate at a hastily organized press conference on the courthouse steps. "This bankruptcy is not a reflection of failure," she said, pausing for emphasis, "but of persecution. What we've created here was visionary—disrupted by a media witch hunt and hostile regulators who never understood the future."

Behind her, her legal team stood motionless. They, too, had seen the numbers.

The Chapter 11 filing was more than a legal mechanism—it was an autopsy in motion. Internal court documents painted a gruesome portrait of a financial house of cards: over $60 million in debt, including undisclosed offshore liabilities and unpaid bonuses masked through shell entities. The ledger included not only deferred player salaries and disputed crypto-based compensation but also unpaid invoices from tech vendors, security firms, and the very law firms now handling the defense. Some contracts bore clauses written in legal code so obscure that even the bankruptcy judge paused during hearings to ask, "What exactly is a disbursement optimization vector?"

It was a humiliation both public and precise.

Every player's contract was now subject to bankruptcy review. Court-appointed financial overseers began combing through clauses related to offshore payment trusts and EBT bonus schemes. Some were deemed "potentially fraudulent instruments of compensation," while others were so convoluted that a special panel of forensic accountants had to be brought in to interpret them.

Still, Marissa Boyd refused to retreat quietly.

Within days, she appeared on KAKE-TV, her voice calm but simmering. "What we did was legal. What we did was smart," she said. "And now they punish us for being ahead of our time. The league, the regulators, even our fans—they've been manipulated by media sensationalism." On ABC's *Prime Focus*, she doubled down, accusing federal agencies of sexism and regional bias. "If this were Silicon Valley," she said, "I'd be hailed as a pioneer. But in Wichita? I'm a pariah."

The public wasn't convinced. And neither were her executives.

In private, the exodus began.

One by one, Boyd's inner circle announced resignations. Her chief financial officer "stepped down for personal reasons." Her head of operations posted a cryptic farewell on LinkedIn. Even her longtime legal advisor left the firm. Within three weeks, the executive floor of PrairieTech Arena stood hollow— offices dark, doors closed, voices silent.

Yet the team staggered forward.

The bankruptcy court allowed limited operations to continue under strict oversight. An independent trustee was appointed—former state auditor

Franklin Bellamy—tasked with reviewing every transaction, approving player stipends, and cutting unnecessary expenditures. Game-day budgets were slashed. Travel arrangements downgraded. Vendors were told payment would be "reviewed upon stabilization," though many never saw another dollar.

The team, once the pride of Kansas, now practiced in silence and played before half-empty stands. Gone was the music. Gone was the fanfare. The roar of adoring fans had become a whispering echo of betrayal.

Player morale plummeted. Practices grew erratic. Coaching sessions, once structured and spirited, turned tense and fragmented. Rumors spread that players were seeking loopholes to break contracts. Others openly consulted agents about transfers. Gabriela Hernandez was spotted at an international airport during a match week. Alyssa Garrett, once the team's heart, stopped wearing the captain's armband entirely.

The locker room had fractured beyond repair.

Off the field, the unraveling accelerated. Corporate sponsors terminated contracts, citing "brand integrity concerns." Promotional events were canceled without rescheduling. Stadium banners were pulled. Merch booths shuttered, their shelves still stacked with jerseys that no one wanted to buy anymore.

Worse still, lawsuits began to flood the team's inbox.

Former employees. Freelancers. Vendors left unpaid. A regional software firm sued for breach of contract, citing a $400,000 balance on custom-built player monitoring platforms. A janitorial services provider filed suit after two months of unpaid invoices. The *Wichita Eagle* published new findings tying Boyd's Silicon Prairie initiatives to undisclosed equity schemes and questionable lobbying efforts.

In Washington, tax authorities widened their investigation. Grand jury subpoenas were now openly discussed on the news. DOJ officials began reviewing whether the bankruptcy filing itself had included willful misstatements—a charge that could escalate the case from civil to criminal.

The entire foundation groaned beneath the weight of its deceit.

Behind closed doors, the Prairie Stars board of directors convened for an emergency session. The independent trustee was blunt: the current operations were unsustainable. Liquid assets were nearly gone. Revenue streams were frozen. The restructuring plan had failed to inspire confidence from sponsors, players, or regulators.

Talk shifted toward Chapter 7—liquidation.

Documents leaked the following week confirmed what insiders already feared: the league had begun drafting contingency plans for the team's dissolution. Player contracts were being reviewed for relocation logistics. The commissioner held private meetings with ownership groups in Chicago and Denver, assessing how to absorb displaced talent. The Prairie Stars were becoming an endangered species.

In one final image, haunting in its simplicity, Boyd stood alone in the skybox of PrairieTech Arena during a home game. Below her, the seats were patchy, the chants muted, the scoreboard irrelevant. A glass of untouched bourbon rested on the sill. She didn't speak. She didn't wave. She simply stared at what once was hers, and what now slipped from her grip like sand through trembling fingers.

The Chapter 11 filing had bought time.

But the collapse was no longer theoretical.

It was happening—on paper, on television, in the hearts of a once-believing city.

And the end was drawing near.

11

From Champions to Collapse

The final blow came not from a stadium chant or a viral video, but from two starkly worded press releases—one from the Kansas Department of Revenue and the other from the Internal Revenue Service. Both were precise, clinical, and devastating. After nearly a year of scrutiny, subpoenas, and forensic tracing, regulators formally concluded their investigations. Their findings left no room for ambiguity.

The Wichita Prairie Stars had committed fraud.

The documents told a story of dual ledgers—one public, one secret—painstakingly kept disguising the flow of deferred compensation. Offshore accounts in the Cayman Islands, Singapore, and Belize funneled millions in bonuses, skirting disclosure requirements and sidestepping domestic taxation. Legal memos uncovered during the probe showed a clear intent to obfuscate liability. At one point, a compliance officer wrote, *"We're building this on sand, and someone's going to notice eventually."*

They had.

Violations of both state and federal tax law were confirmed, including willful misrepresentation, tax evasion, conspiracy to defraud the government, and failure to disclose foreign asset holdings. The words landed like lead across the country. For those who had once cheered for the Kansas Miracle, the dream had turned fully, finally, into dust.

Within hours, *ESPN* dropped its long-awaited investigative documentary:

From Champions to Collapse. Narrated in haunting tones and interspersed with interviews, drone footage, and financial breakdowns, it pulled no punches. Viewers watched as graphics charted the flow of money through trust networks, as former interns described whispered fears, and as tax experts explained how seemingly legal tactics crossed into illegal territory. A now-famous clip played over and over: the moment a board member admitted, *"We knew we were riding the line. We just didn't know when it would snap."*

It had snapped, and the sound reverberated nationally.

ABC News, KAKE-TV, and every major outlet covered the fallout daily. Morning shows hosted panels with sports economists and white-collar crime attorneys. The "Timeline of the EBT Scheme" ran every hour on ESPN, from Marissa Boyd's takeover in 2028 to the team's impending implosion in 2033. The narrative arc was mythic glory built on deceit, the American Dream in cleats and neon lights, reduced to a parable of greed.

In the aftermath, the players began to speak.

Alyssa Garrett, once the soul of the team, appeared on ESPN's *Outside the Lines.* Her voice shook only slightly as she described the disintegration from the inside. "We were told we were part of something revolutionary," she said, eyes heavy with disillusionment. "We believed in it. In her. But what she built... it wasn't a miracle. It was a mask." Her words were raw, unpolished, and devastating.

Gabriela Hernandez, who had remained silent since her contract leak, gave a moving interview to *60 Minutes.* She spoke of feeling used, paraded, and ultimately betrayed. "They knew we trusted them. And they weaponized that trust," she said, tears brimming. "I thought I was building a legacy. But I was just a headline waiting to happen."

Behind the scenes, staff began to disappear. Some quietly resigned. Others were let go in shadowed HR meetings as audit revelations made their positions untenable. No farewell parties. No press releases. Just a trail of cleared desks and unforwarded emails. Those who stayed walked through the halls with eyes lowered and doors half-shut.

Inside the locker room, what remained was no longer a team.

It was a splintered mosaic of silence, suspicion, and fatigue. Players who had once danced and sung before matches now arrived in silence, dressed quickly, and left without speaking. Staff walked on eggshells, unsure who was next to go or who might still be cooperating with investigators. Some players packed their belongings weeks before the final match, operating on instinct that this was the end—no formal send-off, no celebratory lap, just a slow, unspoken dissolution.

Stadiums, once electric with standing-room-only crowds, now echoed with absence. The final games were more eulogy than sport. Protest signs lined the gates—*"This Isn't What We Cheered For"*, *"Boyd Built a Lie"*, *"Justice for the Players."* Fans, once feverishly loyal, arrived only to boo or burn old jerseys. Others stayed home, their silence louder than the chants. Entire sections of PrairieTech Arena were cordoned off due to low attendance. The merchandise booths shut early—most products now marked 80% off or quietly removed altogether.

Sponsors didn't wait for the final whistle.

Major national brands pulled funding. Local partnerships dissolved overnight. Television contracts were reevaluated. The team's final press conference was sparsely attended and mercifully short. No player wanted to speak. No executive remained willing to take questions. And no one, not the city, not the league, not even the players—believed the team could be salvaged.

Wichita, once so proud, turned bitter.

Civic leaders who had praised Boyd at ribbon-cuttings now publicly condemned her. A city councilwoman labeled the scandal "an embarrassment to our institutions." Former boosters released statements expressing "profound regret" for their support. The term *Kansas Miracle* was now spoken with a sneer, if at all.

And the league, though not indicted, wasn't spared.

Critics questioned how a professional sports body could allow such financial opacity to fester unchecked. Congressional aides began whispering about broader reforms. Editorials ran in national newspapers, demanding increased oversight of compensation practices and tighter scrutiny of emerging sports franchises.

Marissa Boyd, once Silicon Prairie's golden child, vanished from public view. No final address. No admission of guilt. No apology.

Only silence.

And in that silence, the echo of collapse stretched endlessly across fields once filled with cheers, across boardrooms once filled with bluster, across a nation once inspired.

The Prairie Stars became more than a scandal.

They became a warning. A monument to ambition unmoored from ethics.

A dynasty dissolved—not by defeat, but by truth.

12

Chapter 7 Conversion

The ruling arrived on a cold December morning, sealing the fate everyone—players, fans, executives, regulators—had known was coming. The U.S. Bankruptcy Court for the District of Kansas, citing "irrevocable financial fraud, unfeasible reorganization, and profound mismanagement," issued a formal order converting the Wichita Prairie Stars' Chapter 11 case into a Chapter 7 liquidation. The decision, drafted in unflinching legal prose, marked the legal death of a team that once stood as the beacon of women's sports ambition.

The final sentence read like an epitaph:

"All operations of the Wichita Prairie Stars shall cease immediately. Assets will be surrendered for liquidation, and all contracts are deemed void effective immediately."

Within hours, news anchors across the nation picked up the story. ESPN led with: *"From Legends to Liquidation: Wichita Falls."* KAKE-TV's headlines were more personal: *"City's Heartbroken Goodbye."* Outside PrairieTech Arena, once a futuristic monument to Marissa Boyd's dream, cameras gathered as a court-appointed trustee posted the official notice on the locked glass doors. The words beneath the bold federal seal were: *"This property is under liquidation supervision. Trespassing is prohibited."*

The dissolution began without ceremony.

An independent trustee—James Corley, a former federal liquidation officer—

was appointed to oversee the asset selloff. Auction schedules were announced with chilling efficiency: stadium lighting rigs, training equipment, audio systems, team buses, office chairs, servers, trophies, and signed memorabilia. Even the digital rights to the Prairie Stars brand, their logo, and merchandise designs were bundled for intellectual property bidding.

By week's end, the clubhouse was shuttered. Staff arrived to find their credentials disabled, their email accounts wiped. Offices once filled with blueprints and optimism were stripped bare. The team's iconic mural in the media wing—depicting three championship stars above the Kansas plains— was painted over by order of the court.

Player contracts, including those of Alyssa Garrett and Gabriela Hernandez, were declared null. The NAWL's central office issued an emergency bulletin formally releasing all players from their agreements. No transition packages. No severance. Only a notification:

"Due to the conversion of the Prairie Stars' bankruptcy case, your contract is hereby terminated. Claims for unpaid wages may be filed through the assigned bankruptcy trustee."

Social media is filled with heartbreak.

Alyssa Garrett posted a photo of her empty locker, her boots hanging by their laces on a hook. *"This place raised me. It also broke me."* Gabriela Hernandez released a video—teary-eyed, shot from her home—announcing her retirement from professional soccer. "I gave everything I had," she said, "but I can't go on. Not after this."

The final game had been played weeks earlier, but its memory now took on a mythic weight.

That day, the stadium had been packed—not with corporate guests or scouts, but with fans who knew the end had come. Black ribbons were tied around stadium railings. Protest signs gave way to handwritten tributes and silent weeping. Before kickoff, players formed a circle, heads bowed in a moment of silence that stretched beyond a mere gesture—it was a mourning. The match itself was sluggish, dreamlike. After the whistle blew, the team gathered once more at midfield and laid their jerseys in a ring—symbols of identity, abandoned and honored all at once.

The photos went viral.

In the weeks that followed, national publications released retrospectives on the Prairie Stars' rise and collapse. *The Atlantic* called them "the Icarus of American sports." *Sports Illustrated* featured a two-page spread: Boyd on one side, the crumbling arena on the other. KAKE ran a local feature titled *"Our Fallen Stars,"* profiling community members—vendors, interns, school partners—whose lives had been intertwined with the franchise.

And then, they were gone.

From the league's website. From the upcoming schedules. From social media directories. The Prairie Stars ceased to exist as a legal entity. Their merchandise was pulled from stores. Their presence was scrubbed from promotional materials. All that remained was memory and mourning.

In Wichita, the grief was tangible. Children who once wore Stars jerseys to school now asked why their team had disappeared. Local businesses reported financial strain from canceled events and halted foot traffic. Youth soccer leagues, once funded by Prairie Stars outreach, scrambled to find new backers. Downtown murals depicting Alyssa's championship goal and Gabriela's victory dance were defaced, then slowly repainted into tributes— homages to a time when hope still glowed beneath the floodlights.

And in the boardrooms of the NAWL, the reckoning had only begun.

An emergency summit was convened in late December. Franchise owners, league officials, and regulators met behind closed doors for twelve hours. Financial compliance protocols were overhauled. Internal audits were launched. Clubs scrambled to update documentation and prepare voluntary disclosures. Legal advisors whispered of other teams "flirting with similar strategies."

Public debate ignited across the nation. Some demanded full league reform, calling for third-party oversight, transparency standards, and whistleblower protections. Others—mostly entrenched figures in the ports business— warned against "overregulation that stifles growth." But no one could deny the truth: the Wichita Prairie Stars had changed everything.

Not through their championships. Not through their fanbase.

But through their fall.

In the end, the stars did not fade.

They imploded.

And their light, too bright and too bold, became a cautionary blaze across the skies of American sports history.

Epilogue: A Cautionary Legacy

The final chapter of the Prairie Stars saga did not close in a stadium, nor under the lights of a press conference, but in the cold formality of a federal courtroom.

In February 2034, Marissa Boyd stood before a judge as the Department of Justice formally unsealed an indictment spanning over forty pages. She was charged with multiple federal counts: wire fraud, tax evasion, and conspiracy to defraud the United States. The charges were comprehensive and unrelenting—each clause anchored by evidence gathered from a yearlong investigation that left no server unturned, no ledger unchecked.

A joint press conference between the DOJ and the IRS drew national attention. Flanked by legal analysts and treasury officials, the U.S. Attorney for the District of Kansas spoke plainly.

"This case is not only about a single sports franchise. It is about the integrity of our financial systems, and the consequences of unchecked ambition masquerading as innovation."

The press conference sparked a wave of reckoning throughout the world of athletics. What had once seemed unthinkable—a professional sports dynasty unraveling under the weight of its deceit—was now a grim precedent.

But amid the collapse, voices of redemption rose.

Alyssa Garrett, whose silence had spoken volumes during the darkest days of the scandal, emerged into the public light with purpose. In a moving op-ed published in *The Players' Tribune*, she wrote:

"I was part of something historic—and something harmful. It took everything I had to accept both truths. But I refuse to let our downfall be the final word."

Alyssa founded *Athletes for Accountability*, a nonprofit dedicated to financial literacy and legal transparency for young athletes. The organization quickly gained traction across NCAA campuses and was lauded for its work in educating student-athletes on contract negotiations, offshore risks, and whistleblower protections. Her voice, once confined to the midfield, now echoed through hearing rooms on Capitol Hill. She testified before Congress in April 2034, urging legislators to pass sweeping reforms in sports finance.

And sitting behind her during that testimony was the woman who made it all possible.

Elena Castillo, the whistleblower, had become a national symbol of conscience. Her name—once whispered in locker rooms and media speculation—was now spoken with respect. Ethics panels invited her to speak. University halls filled to hear her reflect on the decision that changed her life—and the lives of so many others. Documentaries featured her with reverence, not as a martyr, but as a compass: a person who chose principle over safety.

In June, Elena passed the bar. Her focus? Sports compliance and whistleblower advocacy. She joined a growing movement of young lawyers determined to ensure that what happened in Wichita would never happen again.

As the dust settled, Sara Trent reemerged—not just as a journalist, but as the author of a story that would define a generation. Her book, *Prairie Mirage: The Fall of the Kansas Model*, debuted to rave reviews. Critics praised its narrative depth, its relentless clarity, and its emotional intelligence. *The New York Times* called it "a masterwork of sports investigative journalism." It topped bestseller lists for weeks, sparking book tours, lecture series, and invitations to international forums on media integrity.

She accepted her awards with grace, but always redirected the spotlight.

"This story was never mine alone," she said at the National Press Club. *"It belonged to a whistleblower with courage, players with wounds, and a city with heartbreak."*

The ripple effect spread far beyond Wichita.

The national soccer federation, responding to overwhelming public pressure and media scrutiny, launched a league-wide audit. Every Division I and II club faced a mandatory financial review. Several were fined for minor infractions—early warning signs that now received urgent attention. Policies were rewritten. Structures were dismantled. A new regulatory body was formed within the league, charged with oversight and enforcement.

Most critically, a set of sweeping reforms was enacted:

Firstly, mandatory disclosure of player compensation, including signing bonuses and external incentive structures. Prohibition of offshore trust-based payment schemes, closing the loopholes exploited by the Prairie Stars. Finally, formal whistleblower protection protocols, granting players and staff a path to report misconduct without fear of retaliation.

The reforms were hard-fought, but necessary. The message was clear: the cost of silence was too high.

As for the Prairie Stars, their name would never again appear on a matchday roster. But their story would never be forgotten.

In sports management classrooms and ethics seminars, their downfall was studied meticulously. Business students analyzed the legal blind spots. Young executives watched documentaries that began not with championships, but with red flags. At the newly expanded *National Sports Ethics Museum* in Indianapolis, a permanent exhibit was unveiled: *"From Champions to Collapse: The Rise and Fall of the Wichita Prairie Stars."* Behind a glass case rested a jersey once worn by Alyssa Garrett—folded, faded, and surrounded by documents that told the true story of what lay beneath the miracle.

And outside that exhibit, a quote from Elena Castillo, etched into the wall:

"A dynasty built on lies is still a lie. And the truth, even whispered, can bring down an empire."

The stadium was gone. The brand was erased.

But the legacy—the lesson—would endure for all eternity.

www.ingramcontent.com/pod-product-compliance
Lightning Source LLC
Chambersburg PA
CBHW052144220626
47052CB00005B/1184